CHRISTMAS FUN
WITH
PETER RABBIT ™

Beatrix Potter

CONTENTS

PETER RABBIT'S ADVENT CALENDAR

December is an even more exciting month if you have an Advent Calendar! To make each day a surprise, ask a friend to make this calendar too and then give them to each other as gifts.

You will need:

- a large piece of cardboard, approx. 46 cm by 36 cm (18" by 14")
- coloured paper
- thin ribbon or wool
- a needle
- glue or sticky tape
- green or red paint
- chocolates, sweets and small gifts

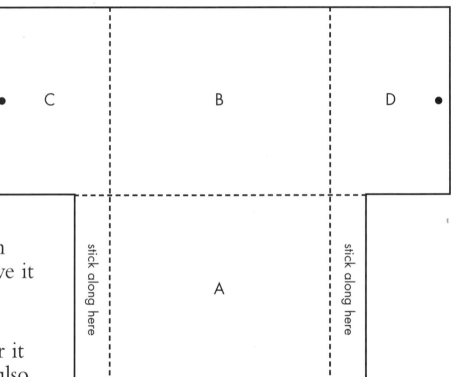

1. Paint the cardboard with green or red paint and leave it to dry.

2. Trace or photocopy the header opposite and colour it in or use paint. You could also use glitter for extra sparkle!

3. Trace the template above. You will need to make 24 of these. Cut them all out in colourful paper.

4. Fold A onto B and use glue or sticky tape to hold it in place, creating a small pouch.

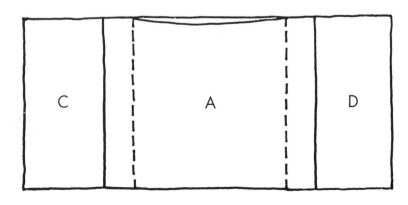

5. Fold C and D into the middle and decorate in any way you choose. Remember to write a number on one of the 'doors' of each pouch, from 1 to 24.

6. Open out flaps C and D, place a sticker on the front of the pouch and put a chocolate, sweet or small gift inside.

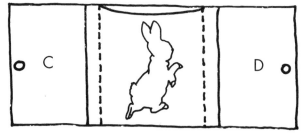

7. Thread the needle with thin ribbon or wool. Push the needle very carefully through C and then out through D. Remove the needle and tie a bow to close the doors of the pouch.

8. Attach each pouch to the cardboard using glue or sticky tape.

PETER RABBIT'S
ADVENT CALENDAR

SPOT THE DIFFERENCE

Tom Thumb and Hunca Munca are stuffing a sixpence into Lucinda and Jane's Christmas stocking. Can you spot five differences between the two pictures? Put a cross by each one.

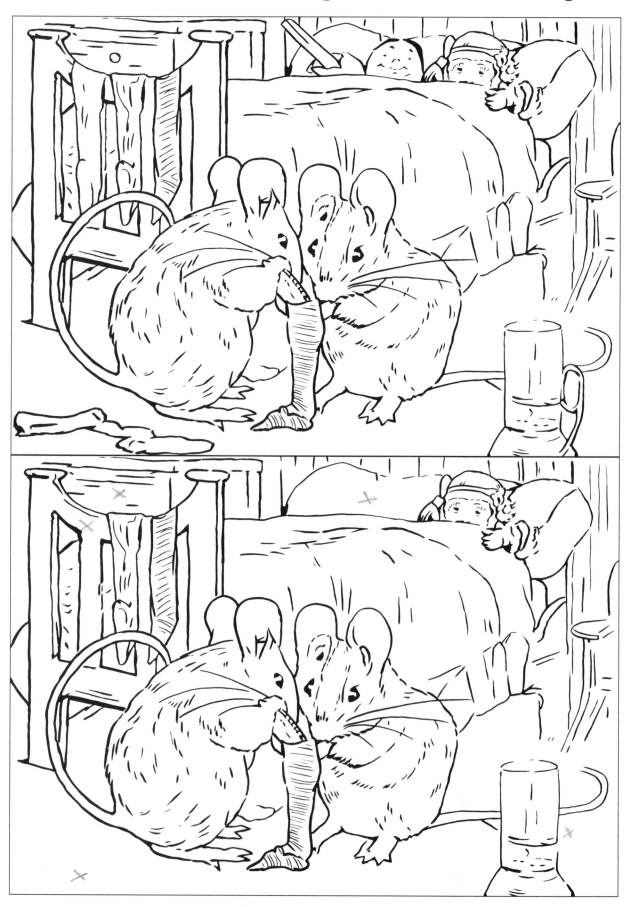

CHRISTMAS SHOPPING

There is so much shopping to do at Christmas! Peter Rabbit and his friends love Ginger and Pickles' village shop because it sells everything they need. How many items can you find in the list below?

sugar
bread
butter
biscuits
milk
camomile tea
herbs
honey
mince pies
nutmeg
potatoes
carrots
onions
apples
oranges
chocolate
candles

A	D	E	O	L	Q	R	H	B	J	W	S	A	T	M
V	U	T	R	X	I	S	E	O	T	A	T	O	P	R
S	B	L	T	F	U	E	A	V	G	P	R	A	C	E
T	U	E	N	G	W	I	M	D	U	L	A	J	F	T
O	H	O	A	B	D	P	Y	K	N	E	P	O	S	T
R	E	R	M	D	A	E	R	B	T	C	P	M	R	U
R	T	A	E	O	J	C	O	E	F	D	L	A	T	B
A	A	N	F	E	N	N	L	R	P	A	E	R	S	H
C	L	G	A	L	H	I	B	S	W	G	S	N	E	L
I	O	E	Y	C	M	M	O	Q	E	U	J	R	I	G
F	C	S	T	O	S	A	I	N	H	L	B	D	E	B
W	O	L	M	T	J	B	F	L	S	S	D	M	V	A
M	H	A	O	P	E	W	Y	C	K	M	T	N	R	E
D	C	B	I	S	C	U	I	T	S	U	L	H	A	T
E	K	U	W	F	N	S	H	O	N	E	Y	S	J	C

HIDE N' SEEK

Timmy and Goody Tiptoes are trying to remember where they hid their nuts for the winter. Find the nuts and place a sticker over each one. Then you can colour in the picture.

PETER RABBIT GIFT WRAP

Make Christmas gifts really special with homemade gift wrap! You can use the same method to make matching gift tags and greetings cards.

You will need:

- a pencil
- a craft knife
- pieces of sponge
- masking tape
- poster or acrylic paints
- thin cardboard, 20 cm x 15 cm (8" x 6")
- thick cardboard, 23 cm x 20 cm (9" x 8")
- tracing paper, 19 cm x 14 cm (7½" x 5½")
- strong thin paper or tissue paper
- paper towels
- newspaper
- a saucer

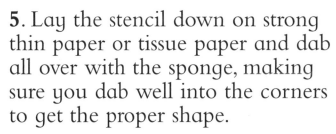

1. Trace the Peter Rabbit stencil.

2. Tape the thin piece of cardboard onto the thick piece and tape the tracing paper on top. Go over the lines of the stencil firmly, making an impression on the cardboard.

3. Remove the tracing paper. Ask an adult to help you to cut out the shapes of the stencil (in the thin piece of cardboard) with a craft knife.

4. Pour some poster or acrylic paint into a saucer. Dab the sponge into the paint.

5. Lay the stencil down on strong thin paper or tissue paper and dab all over with the sponge, making sure you dab well into the corners to get the proper shape.

6. Lift the stencil off carefully. Wipe the back of the stencil clean and place it somewhere else on the paper.

7. Repeat this method with the radish stencil.

TRIMMING THE TREE

Decorating the Christmas tree is an exciting tradition which can be even more fun if you make your own trims.

MRS TIGGY-WINKLE'S TASTY BUNDLES

These pretty bundles are filled with festive treats!

You will need:

- ribbon
- a selection of nuts, raisins and candy
- circles of material, approx. 10 cm (4") in diameter

1. Cut out several small circles of material and lay them pattern side down on a flat surface.

2. Place some 'festive treats' in the centre of each circle, gather together the ends of the material and tie with a length of ribbon to form a small bundle.

3. Tie each bundle onto a branch of your tree and try very hard to keep your hands off them until Christmas Day!

POPCORN AND CRANBERRY STRINGS

Always make double the amount of popcorn you think you'll need—it's impossible not to eat it while you're making these!

You will need:

- un-popped or ready-made popcorn (uncoated)
- fresh cranberries
- needle and thread

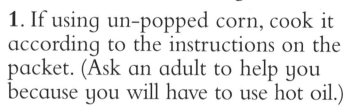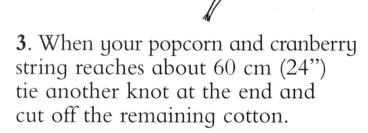

1. If using un-popped corn, cook it according to the instructions on the packet. (Ask an adult to help you because you will have to use hot oil.)

2. Tie a knot at the end of the thread and string on the berries and corn alternately.

3. When your popcorn and cranberry string reaches about 60 cm (24") tie another knot at the end and cut off the remaining cotton.

4. Arrange the string around the branches of your Christmas tree for a lovely glowing decoration.

HUNCA MUNCA'S MINI STOCKINGS

You could place small gifts inside these stockings
for extra surprises on Christmas Day!

You will need: (for one mini stocking)

- a piece of felt, approx. 22 cm (8.5") square
- paper, scissors, a pen
- fabric glue
- a needle and a few pins
- sequins, ribbon and embroidery thread

1. Fold the felt square in half. Draw a stocking shape on a piece of paper, cut it out and pin it to the felt square.

2. Cut round the shape and then unpin it so that you are left with two felt stocking shapes.

3. Pin the two pieces together and sew the outside edges together in blanket stitch (except for the top edges!).

4. Stick on some sequins using the fabric glue. Sew a loop of ribbon onto the top inside corner to hang it up, and then carefully hide a small gift inside!

SNOWFLAKES

You'll be amazed at what beautiful snowflake shapes you can create. And each one will be different, just like real snowflakes!

You will need:

- sheets of medium-weight paper
- glitter
- scissors and glue
- ribbon

1. Draw a circle, using a small plate as a guide, and cut it out. Fold the circle in half and then in half again.

2. Cut out different shapes from the quarter circle and all around the edges. Make the shapes as complicated as you can, but be careful not to cut away all of the edges.

3. Open it out carefully and you should find a beautiful snowflake. Dab on a little glue and sprinkle on some glitter; shake off when the glue is dry.

4. Hang it on your tree using a piece of ribbon.

Hurry Home, Peter!

Peter Rabbit is delivering letters to his friends on his way back to the cosy burrow. Help him find his way, placing a sticker over each letter.

A Festive Feast!

Why not invite some friends round for a Christmas tea party?
These festive snacks are fun to make and delicious to eat!

Tabitha Twitchit's Toasties

These Christmas tree shaped toasties are smothered in melted cheese.
You can decorate them with savoury trimmings!

You will need:
- brown or white sliced bread
  (1 slice makes 1 toastie)
- butter or margarine
- grated cheese
- tomato sauce
- 1 red pepper
- 1 green pepper
- 1 carrot

1. Cut each slice of bread into quarters (diagonally) so that you are left with triangle shapes.

2. Arrange them on a grill pan and toast them on one side under the grill.

3. Spread the uncoated side of each piece with butter or margarine, then a thin layer of tomato sauce. Sprinkle on some grated cheese, taking care not let it spill over the edges. Grill lightly until the cheese melts.

4. While the cheese is still hot, overlap the triangles slightly to form a Christmas tree shape. When the cheese has cooled, the toasties should remain in this shape, though you will need to handle them carefully.

5. Decorate the trees with tiny pieces of red and green pepper, and add a chunk of carrot for the trunk.

Aunt Pettitoes' Chocolate Dip

This recipe is also known as 'Chocolate Fondue'. It can be quite messy but dipping into the chocolate is such fun!

You will need:

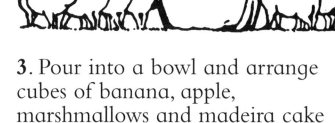

- 4 bananas
- 4 apples
- a small madeira cake
- cocktail sticks
- 300 ml (½ pint) whipping cream
- 400 g (14 oz) plain dessert chocolate
- 50 g (2 oz) unsalted butter
- 6 tbsp pineapple juice
- marshmallows

1. Break the chocolate into pieces and put them into a basin, in a saucepan of simmering water.

2. Melt the chocolate and stir in the cream and pineapple juice. Continue stirring, and when the mixture is smooth stir in the butter a little at a time.

3. Pour into a bowl and arrange cubes of banana, apple, marshmallows and madeira cake on a plate.

4. Now simply dip the cubes into the sauce using the cocktail sticks. Delicious!

Cecily Parsley's Fruity Punch

Warm punch is scrumptious and the floating slices of fruit are a perfect finishing touch.

You will need:

- 1 litre orange juice
- 1 litre apple juice
- 1 litre pineapple juice
- 5 cloves
- a cinnamon stick
- 3 tbsp granulated sugar
- 1 apple
- 1 orange

1. Put the fruit juice into a saucepan with the cloves, cinnamon stick and sugar.

2. Heat and stir until the sugar has melted and the juice is hot but not boiling.

3. Strain the liquid and discard the cloves and cinnamon stick.

4. Pour into a bowl and float sliced apple and orange on the top.

CHRISTMAS CRACKERS

Make these easy crackers and Christmas will
go with a bang!

You will need:

- cardboard roll
- crepe paper (2 colours)
- scissors
- glue
- double-sided adhesive tape
- ribbon and other trimmings
- 'snaps'

1. Cut the cardboard roll to 10cm
(4"). Push a 'snap' through the roll
and tape it in place at one end.
Insert a small gift, a joke and
some sweets.

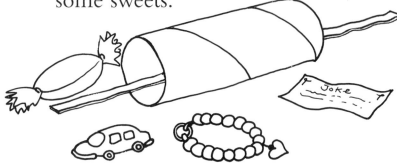

2. Cut a piece of crepe paper,
45 cm (18") in length, and twice
the circumference of the cardboard
roll. Cut another piece of crepe
paper (a different colour),
measuring 20 cm (8") in length
and the circumference of the roll
plus a small overlap. Cut each
end of both pieces of crepe paper
into small zig-zags.

3. Place the cardboard roll in the
centre of the long edge of the crepe
paper and wrap the paper firmly
around it. Secure with tape. Repeat
with the other piece of crepe paper.

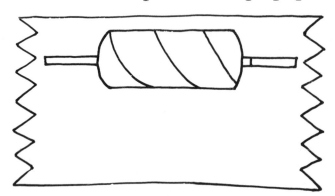

4. Tie a length of ribbon around
each end and ease the knots
towards each end of the cardboard
roll. Tie the ribbon in bows.

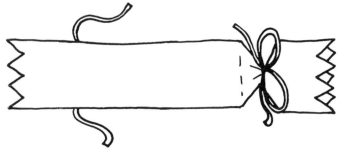

5. Decorate the cracker in any way
you wish. You could use stickers,
sequins, glitter, colourful pens or
perhaps some holly and berries.

14

REBUS LETTER

To read the letter, fill in the missing words by placing the correct stickers over the dotted shapes.

Dear Mrs Tittlemouse,

I am writing to tell you about my naughty sor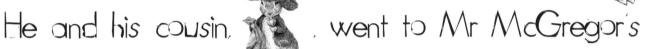

He and his cousin,  . went to Mr McGregor's

garden. They had to be rescued from underneath a

 which a  sat on for five hours!

I have forgiven them this time because Peter has

found his  and

He and Benjamin collected some lovely  for

me. Unfortunately they used my  to carry

them home, so I shall have to send it

to  to be washed.

Yours, Mrs Rabbit

Colouring Fun!

Here are some helpful mice from *The Tailor of Gloucester*, sewing a magnificent coat for the tailor.

CHRISTMAS WISHES

Can you imagine what Peter Rabbit and his friends would wish for at Christmas? Place the correct stickers in each space.

GIFTS TO MAKE

Everybody loves to receive homemade gifts at Christmas, and making them is such fun!

SNOWSTORM

You can use anything that water won't spoil to make the model for this sparkling gift.

You will need:
- model-making material
- silver glitter
- food jar with lid
- glycerine
- all-purpose glue
- water-proof decorations for a snowman

1. Model a snowman on a white mound on the inside of the jar lid, no wider than the mouth of the jar (keep checking that the lid will still screw on).

2. Use small black beads for the snowman's eyes and buttons, a small strip of material for a scarf and anything suitable you can find for a hat. Allow it to dry. (You may have to bake the clay in the oven, but some dry naturally.)

3. Secure the model to the base using all-purpose glue.

4. Half fill the jar with glycerine. Add water until the jar is $\frac{3}{4}$ full. Pour in some glitter.

5. Carefully lower the model into the jar and screw the lid on tightly.

6. Turn the jar the right way up and watch the snow fall!

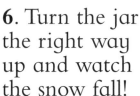

STAINED GLASS NIGHTLIGHT

This nightlight looks so beautiful in a dark room.
Turn to page 24 for the templates.

You will need:

- tracing paper
- black art paper
- coloured tissue paper
- paper glue
- scissors
- pencil
- small glass tumbler or jar
- nightlight

1. Trace one of the templates. Cut it out so that you are left with a long strip which fits around your glass tumbler or jar.

2. Cut a piece of black art paper to the same size and place the tracing paper on top. Trace over the lines firmly so that it makes a clear impression.

3. Cut as shown by the dotted lines. Ask an adult to help you.

4. Cover the gaps with pieces of different coloured tissue paper glued onto the back of the design.

5. When it is dry, wrap the strip around your tumbler or jar and glue the ends together. Place a nightlight inside.

6. Always ask an adult to light the candle for you and remember the safety rules.

PARTY GAMES

These fun party games are sure to keep your guests amused. Perhaps you could also provide prizes for the winners!

MR JEREMY'S FISHING GAME (2+ players)

Poor Mr Jeremy Fisher didn't have any luck when he tried to catch some minnows for his dinner, but you and your friends will have lots of fun with his fishing game!

You will need:

- silver foil
- a length of string, approx. 18cm (7")
- 20 paper clips
- a small magnet
- a straw
- a bowl

How to play

Make 20 fish shapes using silver foil and slide a paper clip onto each of them. Tie one end of the string to the straw and the other end to the magnet to form a fishing rod. Put the fish in a bowl of water. Take it in turns to lift the fish out of the water using the rod, giving each player one minute to get as many as they can; or make several fishing rods and you can all go fishing together!

BENJAMIN BUNNY'S TREASURE HUNT
(2+ players)

Benjamin Bunny loves adventures, and you can have your own adventure at home searching for these treasures!

	Points
Peter Rabbit's tail (a ball of cotton-wool)	10
Mr McGregor's hat	10
Tom Kitten's whisker (a short length of string)	10
Jemima Puddle-duck's egg	9
Benjamin Bunny's onion	9
The Flopsy Bunnies' lettuce leaf	8
Mr Jeremy Fisher's fishing rod (a piece of string tied onto a twig)	8
The Tailor of Gloucester's cotton reel	7
Mrs Tittlemouse's dustpan and brush	7
Squirrel Nutkin's bag of nuts	6
Pigling Bland's peppermints	6
Mrs Tiggy-winkle's washing (three items of clothing)	5
Mrs Rabbit's apron	5

Give each player a list of all the objects.
Ask an adult to hide the objects around the house.
Now begin your treasure hunt! After fifteen minutes,
all players must gather together and show what objects
they have found. Add up everyone's score. The winner is
the player with the highest score, and it is their turn to
hide the objects for the next game.

GREETINGS CARD

Create a stunning Christmas scene with this greetings card. You could draw the picture inside or use a sticker.

THROUGH-THE-WINDOW CARD

You will need:

- thin white card
- black card
- paints or crayons
- a pencil and a ruler
- a craft knife or scissors
- clear all-purpose glue
- cotton wool
- patterned fabric

1. Cut out a piece of white card measuring 25 cm (9") by 16 cm (6") and fold it in half.

2. Using a ruler and a pencil, draw a square on one half of the card, measuring 12 cm (5") by 8 cm (3"). Carefully cut out the square with a craft knife or scissors.

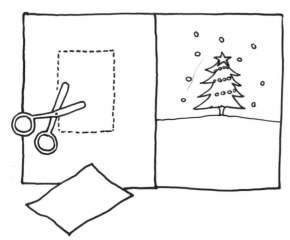

3. Open out the card and draw a picture on the right hand side so that when the card is closed you can see the picture through the window.

4. Make a frame by sticking some black card strips, ½ cm (¼") wide, round the edge of the window and two strips to form a cross in the middle.

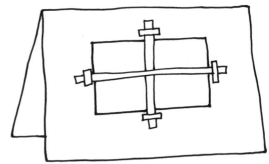

5. Glue some cotton wool along the edges of the window pane as snow.

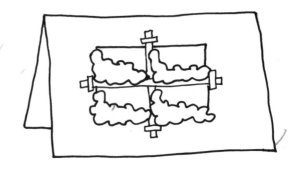

6. Cut out two pieces of fabric, 14 cm (5½") by 3½ cm (1½").

7. Glue the pieces of fabric to the top of the window frame. Pull the middle of each 'curtain' to the sides and stick.

A Dinner Guest

Jemima Puddle-duck has met a sandy-whiskered gentleman while looking for a place to lay her eggs. He has asked her to share supper with him, but Jemima doesn't realize that she is to be the main course! This word puzzle contains nine things for the meal. How many can you find?

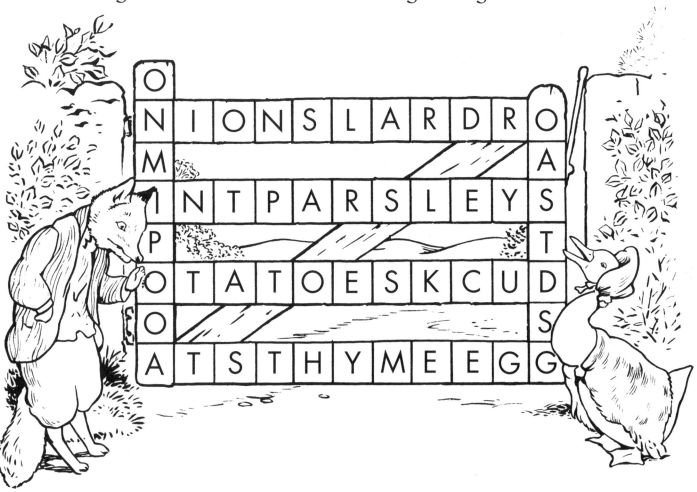

```
O
N I O N S L A R D R O
M                   A
I N T P A R S L E Y S
P                   T
O T A T O E S K C U D
O                   S
A T S T H Y M E E G G
```

Now fill in the first letter of each of the things drawn here to find the name of something Jemima is wearing in the puzzle above.

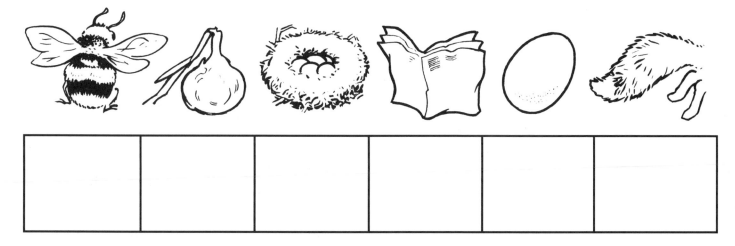

23

TEMPLATES